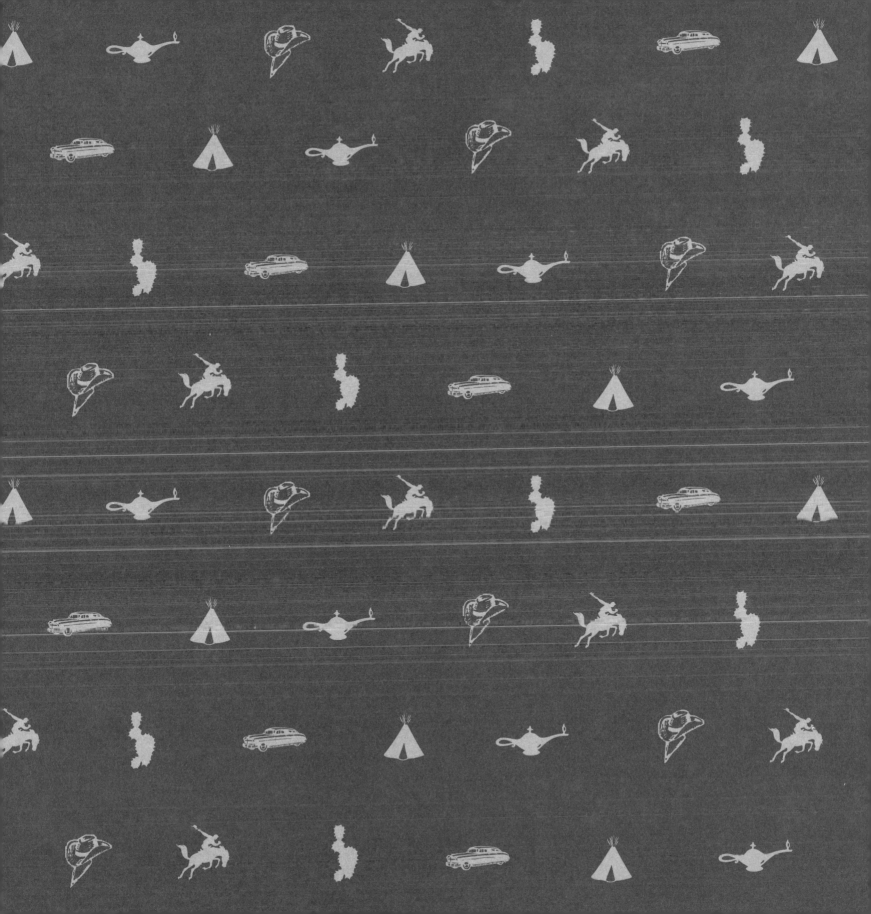

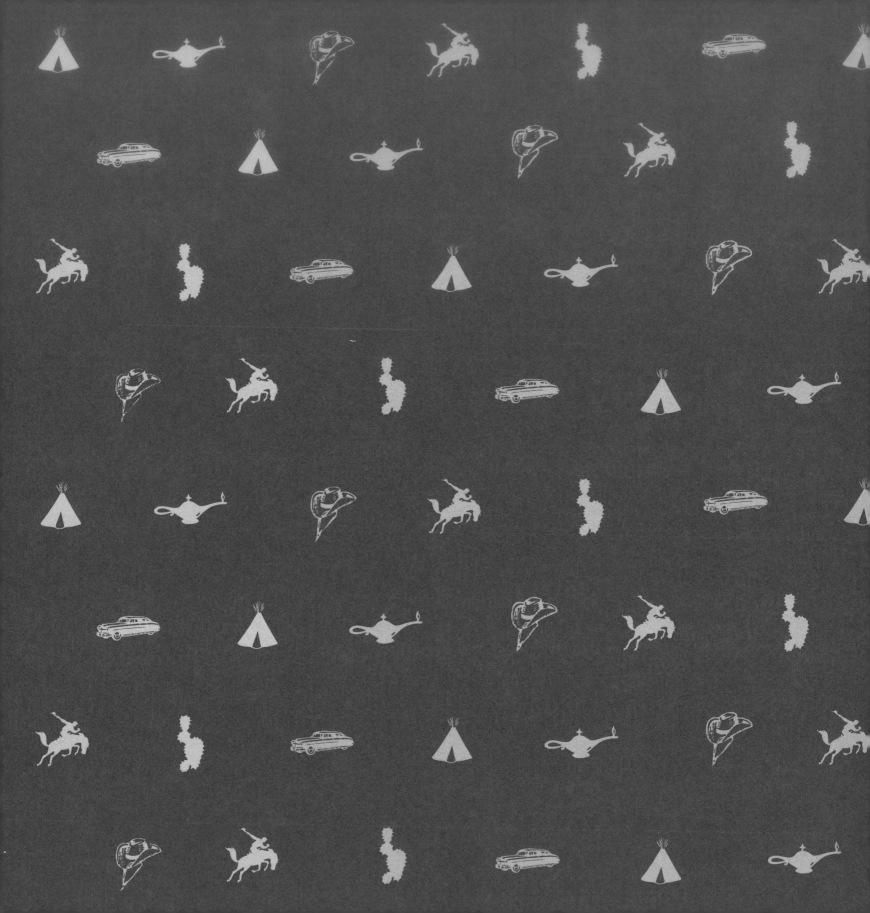

Thomasson-Grant

Charlottesville, Virginia

Backseat Buckaroo

Edward Valfre

Published in 1995
by Thomasson-Grant.
Text and photographs copyright
© 1995 by Edward Valfre.

Any inquiries should be directed to:
Thomasson-Grant, Inc.
One Morton Drive, Suite 500
Charlottesville, Virginia 22903-6806
(804) 977-1780

Printed in Singapore

01 00 99 98 97 96 95   5 4 3 2 1

Library of Congress Cataloging-in-Publication Data

Valfre, Edward.
    Backseat buckaroo / Edward Valfre.
        p. cm.
    Summary: A young boy transforms the landscape he
sees from the backseat of his parents' car into a series of
exciting episodes.
    ISBN 1-56566-078-1
    [1. Automobile travel–Fiction. 2. Imagination–Fiction.]
I. Title.
PZ7.V253Bac 1995
[Fic]–dc20   94-39597
                                                    CIP
                                                    AC

To the memory of my brother, Ben,
and our many travels together
in the backseat of our parents' car.

The backseat of a car
is no place for a buckaroo
who's ready for adventure.

We had driven a million miles from home,
when a blackbird appeared in the road ahead.
It was about to tell us a secret message,
but Dad honked the horn.
The bird flew away and we kept on driving.

The farther we traveled,
the stranger things became.

By my calculations, we were lost.

If we were ever to reach Oklahoma,
we definitely needed some help.
An Indian guide pointed the way,
but warned us to be on the lookout for danger.

Sure as shootin',
trouble was just around the bend.
It was desperadoes of the most dangerous kind.
If they had a sneaky plan, you couldn't tell
from their expressions.
Thanks to some fancy driving by Dad,
we zoomed by without a face-off.

A few miles later, we saw an elephant
making a daring escape
from a roadside carnival.

A carousel horse by the name of Louise
was also tired of carnival life,
and the two of them were headed to Mexico
to sing show tunes in a small cabaret.
They asked me to join, promising we would
become overnight sensations. But I had to say no.
You see, I can't carry a tune,
and I only know one word of Spanish.

A white rabbit began running alongside the car.
"Hey! What's the hurry?" I shouted.
"I'm late! I'm late!" he squeaked. "Just don't forget
to rescue the princess!" And with that,
he disappeared down a rabbit hole
and into a different story.

We passed the castle that held the princess.
I guess you could say that my luck with princesses
hasn't been too good
since I stepped on Sleeping Beauty's foot
in last year's school play.

I was going to need the greatest horse of all time—
one that could ride on the wind,
save the princess, and still keep Dad's schedule
of making Albuquerque by suppertime.

Dinosaurs stood between me and the princess.
They flashed their huge teeth
and gave out a ferocious roar.
But I knew they were bluffing.
I'd seen our dog, Muffy, use this trick a kajillion times.

The dinosaurs agreed to become the star attractions
at a local petting zoo, on the condition that they be fed
huge amounts of ice cream.
With them out of the way, I swept the princess up
onto my horse and carried her to safety.
I could see her eyes giving me that dreamy look,
so I quickly said, "No time for a thank you, Ma'am.
I think I hear my Mom callin'."
I tipped my hat and rode off,
being extra careful to avoid her feet.

We pushed on through the desert.

It was there I laid my eyes on the magic lamp.

Getting a Genie's attention at 60 miles an hour

takes some doing. At the top of my voice,

I shouted out of the car window,

"I've got a jelly sandwich for anyone granting wishes!"

The Genie finally showed up
at a gas station down the road.

"What is your request, Master Buckaroo?" he grumbled.
A friendlier-looking Genie would have been a nice start,
but I didn't want to waste any of my wishes.
I had to be very cunning. After a great deal of thought,
I made my choices:

    1. To ride a bucking bronco.

    2. An extra hour before bedtime.

    3. To someday sleep in a teepee.

I started to believe that my third wish just might come true when my parents began discussing places to spend the night. I ever so casually said, "My, what a lovely variety of teepees in these parts."

There were teepees with television,

teepees with pets,

teepees with local weather information,

and, of course, the ever popular plain teepee.

Just before sundown, we stopped for a snack.

Mom gave me a quarter to spend on anything I wanted.

I decided to spend it on a fortune teller.

I looked at my fortune. Here is what it said:

"You will travel to exotic lands
and have many adventures."

I looked back at the road and knew it was true.

So much had happened in just one day,
and all from the backseat of our car.
As we rolled down the highway,
I yelled out my one Spanish word:

"Adios!"

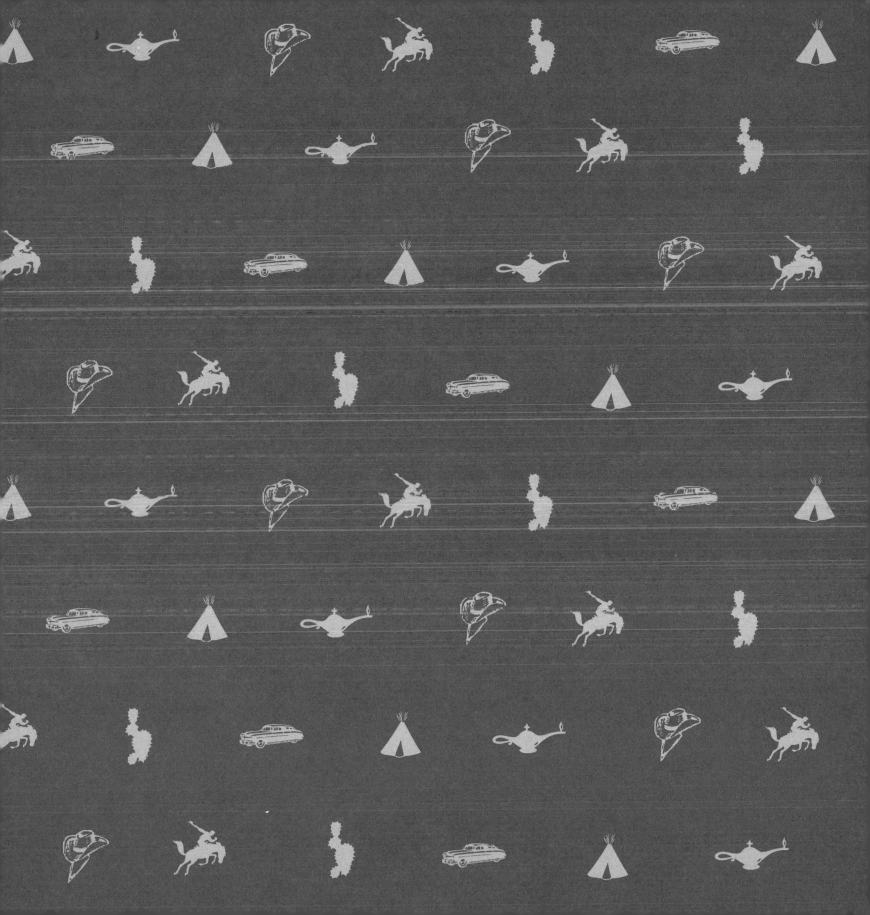